STANLEY CUP
ALL-TIME GREATS

BY ANTHONY STREETER

Book design by Jake Slavik
Cover design by Jake Slavik

Photographs ©: Keith Srakocic/AP Images, cover (top), 1 (top); Mike Ridewood/AP Images, cover (bottom), 1 (bottom); AP Images, 4; Robert Riger/Getty Images Sport/Getty Images, 6; Bettmann/Getty Images, 9; Robert Shaver/Bruce Bennett/Getty Images, 10; Bruce Bennett/Getty Images, 13; Steve Crandall/Getty Images Sport/Getty Images, 14; Graig Abel/Getty Images Sport/Getty Images, 16; John Giamundo/Bruce Bennett/Getty Images, 19; Jonathan Daniel/Getty Images Sport/Getty Images, 21

Press Box Books, an imprint of Press Room Editions.

ISBN
978-1-63494-863-0 (library bound)
978-1-63494-881-4 (paperback)
978-1-63494-916-3 (epub)
978-1-63494-899-9 (hosted ebook)

Library of Congress Control Number: 2023923049

Distributed by North Star Editions, Inc.
2297 Waters Drive
Mendota Heights, MN 55120
www.northstareditions.com

Printed in the United States of America
082024

ABOUT THE AUTHOR

Anthony Streeter is a former sportswriter who has written for various newspapers. He lives in Columbia, Missouri, with his wife and three kids.

TABLE OF CONTENTS

KENNEDY
10

CHAPTER 1
EARLY STARS

The Stanley Cup was first awarded in 1893. At first, Canadian amateur teams competed for the trophy. Then, in the 1926–27 season, the National Hockey League (NHL) took control of the Cup. The league's champion still gets to lift the Stanley Cup today.

The Toronto Maple Leafs were the NHL's first dynasty. **Ted Kennedy** was a big reason why. The playmaking center led the Leafs to five titles from 1945 to 1951. He was Toronto's captain for two of those seasons. Kennedy always seemed to score a big goal when the Leafs needed it most.

The Detroit Red Wings dominated the early 1950s. **Ted Lindsay** played in eight Stanley Cup Finals, winning four. The left winger was known for his toughness. He could also score. His four goals in Game 2 of the 1955 Final set a record for the NHL era.

No NHL team has won more championships than the Montreal Canadiens. Ten of them came between 1943 and 1967. That was the NHL's "Original Six" era. The league doubled in size in 1967–68. Yet Montreal added another eight titles from 1968 to 1979. Canadiens center **Henri Richard** lifted the Cup 11 times. No player has won more championships. Center **Jean Beliveau** and right winger **Yvan Cournoyer** each won 10. However, Montreal's biggest star might have been right winger **Maurice Richard**. Known as the

STAT SPOTLIGHT

STANLEY CUP FINAL RECORD

CAREER GOALS

Maurice Richard: 34

"Rocket," he was the league's most dangerous scorer. And in 1957, he tied Lindsay by scoring four goals in one game.

Of course, other teams won titles too. **Bobby Orr** was the league's best defenseman for years. On top of playing stellar defense, Orr could start attacking plays or finish them off. He famously scored the Cup-winning goal in 1970 for the Boston Bruins. Then he did it again two years later.

The Philadelphia Flyers won the Stanley Cup in both 1974 and 1975. Hard-working center **Bobby Clarke** was the heart and soul

TOE BLAKE

Toe Blake was a high-scoring winger for 13 seasons with the Canadiens. Injuries ended his playing career in 1948. But Blake returned in 1955 as the team's coach. Blake was strict. He was also a master strategist. In 1968, Blake retired as an 11-time champion. Eight of those wins came as a coach.

of those teams. But **Bernie Parent** shined brightest on the big stage. The goalie posted shutouts in Game 6 of both series to secure the Cup. And he earned the Conn Smythe Trophy as the postseason's Most Valuable Player (MVP) both years.

DRYDEN
29
CANADIEN

CHAPTER 2

CLASSIC PERFORMERS

Ken Dryden played in just six games during the 1970–71 season. Then the playoffs started. The Montreal Canadiens named Dryden their starting goalie. Before long, the rookie was red hot. His elite ability to stop shots led Montreal to the championship. Then he won five more through 1979.

A new dynasty took over the next season. The New York Islanders won four straight Stanley Cups. **Bryan Trottier** and **Mike Bossy** led the way. Trottier, a center, had no weaknesses in his game. In 1980, his scoring sparked a championship run. And few players in NHL history could find the net like Bossy. The right winger scored 17 goals in 23 Cup Final games. That included a hat trick to open the 1982 series. Bossy also scored the Cup-winning goal in both 1982 and 1983.

The Islanders nearly won a fifth championship in 1984. Instead, they ran into a young center named **Wayne Gretzky**. His playmaking ability was legendary. He would go on to shatter the league's scoring records. And behind "The Great One," the Edmonton Oilers

STAT SPOTLIGHT

STANLEY CUP FINAL RECORD

POINTS IN A SERIES

Wayne Gretzky: 13 (1988)

won four Cups from 1984 to 1988. In the 1985 Final, Gretzky scored seven goals in five games. In 1988, his 10 assists led the way.

Several talented teammates helped Gretzky. Perhaps none were more important than **Mark Messier**. Edmonton's captain won four titles alongside Gretzky. Then he led the team to another in 1990, after the Oilers traded Gretzky. Teammates were drawn to Messier as a leader. That leadership showed in 1994. By then, Messier had joined the New York Rangers.

LEMIEUX
66

Behind their confident captain, the Rangers won their first Cup in 54 years.

Injuries slowed **Mario Lemieux** at times. The Pittsburgh Penguins center played in just 26 games in 1990–91. But when Lemieux was healthy, his unique offensive skills were nearly unstoppable. In the 1991 playoffs, Lemieux won the Conn Smythe Trophy while leading the Penguins to their first championship. He was back again in 1992. Lemieux scored five goals in the Final, and two of them were game-winners. It was no surprise when he won another Conn Smythe.

SCOTTY BOWMAN

A head injury ended Scotty Bowman's dreams of becoming a pro hockey player. Instead, he became the NHL's most successful coach. Bowman led five teams over 30 seasons. He set all-time coaching records with 1,244 wins and nine Stanley Cups.

ROY
33
KOHO

CHAPTER 3

MODERN LEGENDS

The Montreal Canadiens called on another rookie goalie in 1986. **Patrick Roy** was so good that fans started calling him "Saint Patrick." At the age of 20, Roy became the youngest Conn Smythe Trophy winner. And he was only getting started. Another Cup and Conn Smythe followed in 1993. In the middle of

STAT SPOTLIGHT

STANLEY CUP FINAL RECORD

MOST SAVES IN A GAME

Patrick Roy: 63 (Game 4, 1996)

the 1995–96 season, the Colorado Avalanche traded for Roy. A few months later, he helped Colorado win its first Cup.

The 2001 Final featured an epic goalie battle. **Martin Brodeur** had already led the New Jersey Devils to a pair of championships. But this time, Roy outdueled him. Roy earned two shutouts in the Final. He also earned his record third Conn Smythe. The Devils were back in 2003, though. This time, Brodeur wouldn't be denied. He tied an NHL record with three shutouts in the series. One came

THE STANLEY CUP

Many people consider the Stanley Cup to be the most famous trophy in sports. Several traditions surround it. One is that every winning player gets to lift the Cup on the ice. The captain usually goes first. One exception came in 2001. Colorado Avalanche defenseman Ray Bourque got the honor. He won his first Cup in his 22nd and final season.

in Game 7 as Brodeur stopped all 24 shots he faced to win the Devils another Cup.

The Detroit Red Wings also won three championships during this era. Center **Steve Yzerman** was the team's leader. The two-way star drove Detroit to a win in 1997. It was the team's first championship in 42 years. Behind their respected captain, the Red Wings won again in 1998 and 2002.

In 2009, **Sidney Crosby** led the Pittsburgh Penguins to their first championship in years. At just 21 years old, Crosby was the youngest captain in league history to lift the Stanley Cup. He only got better after that. The superstar center led the Penguins to titles in 2016 and 2017. His stellar play earned him the Conn Smythe both years.

During the 2010s, two players led the charge in Chicago. Center **Jonathan Toews** had grit, skill, and poise. The Blackhawks named him captain when he was only 20. Meanwhile, right winger **Patrick Kane** dominated games with his playmaking and scoring. Together they led Chicago to three championships from 2010 to 2015. Each won a Conn Smythe.

The salary cap now makes it hard to keep good teams together for long. Back-to-back championships are rare. But a dominant goalie can help overcome that.

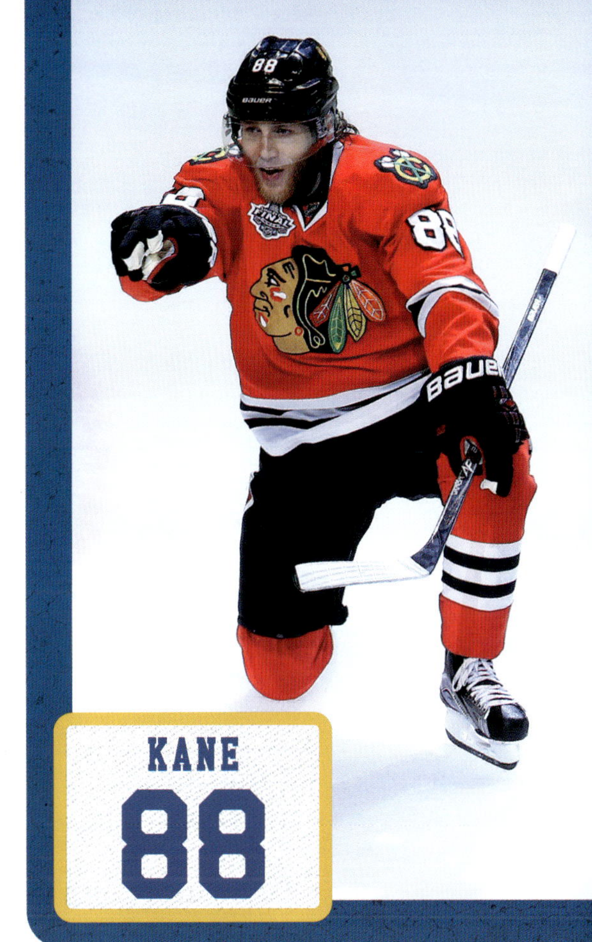

Andrei Vasilevskiy proved it in Tampa Bay. He led the Lightning to three straight Finals. They won in 2020 and 2021. In 2021, he stopped 132 of 140 shots over five games. Lightning fans hoped he would lead the team to even more Stanley Cup victories in the future.

TIMELINE

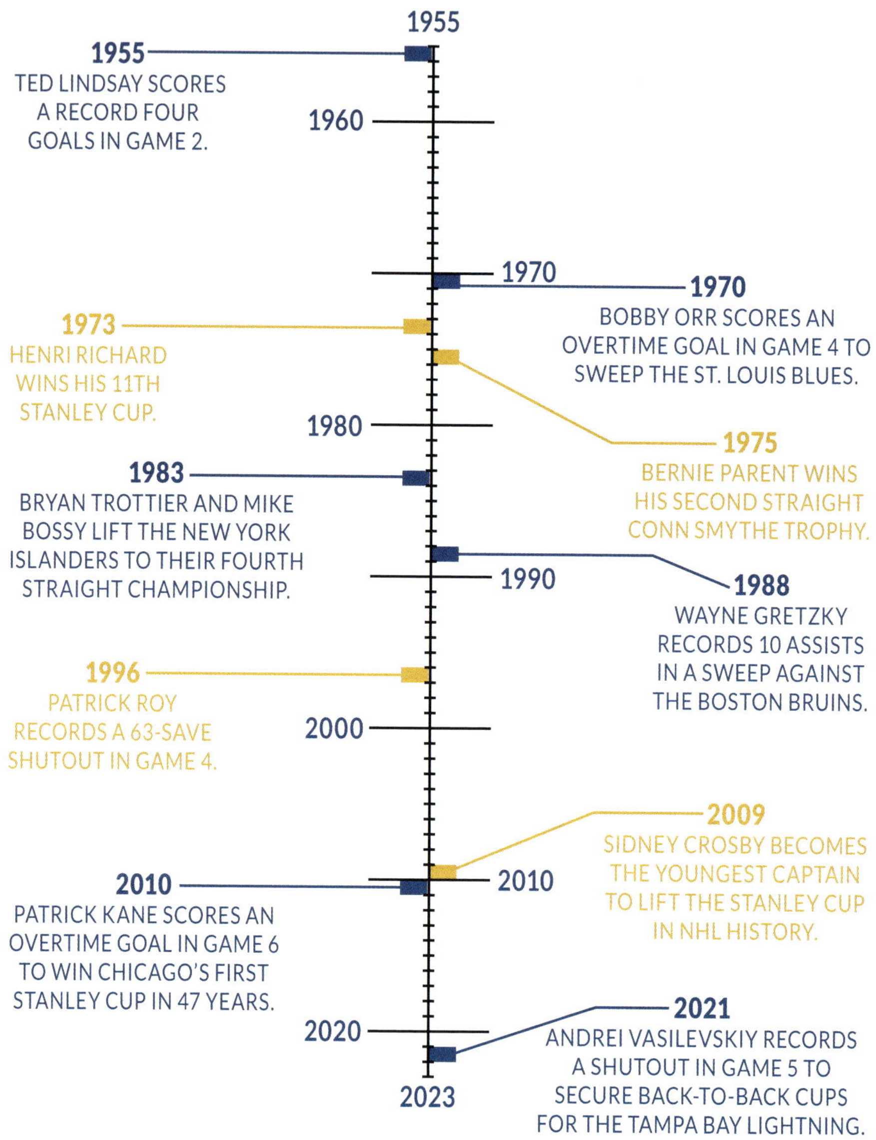

1955
1955
TED LINDSAY SCORES A RECORD FOUR GOALS IN GAME 2.
1960
1970
1970
BOBBY ORR SCORES AN OVERTIME GOAL IN GAME 4 TO SWEEP THE ST. LOUIS BLUES.
1973
HENRI RICHARD WINS HIS 11TH STANLEY CUP.
1975
BERNIE PARENT WINS HIS SECOND STRAIGHT CONN SMYTHE TROPHY.
1980
1983
BRYAN TROTTIER AND MIKE BOSSY LIFT THE NEW YORK ISLANDERS TO THEIR FOURTH STRAIGHT CHAMPIONSHIP.
1988
WAYNE GRETZKY RECORDS 10 ASSISTS IN A SWEEP AGAINST THE BOSTON BRUINS.
1990
1996
PATRICK ROY RECORDS A 63-SAVE SHUTOUT IN GAME 4.
2000
2009
SIDNEY CROSBY BECOMES THE YOUNGEST CAPTAIN TO LIFT THE STANLEY CUP IN NHL HISTORY.
2010
2010
PATRICK KANE SCORES AN OVERTIME GOAL IN GAME 6 TO WIN CHICAGO'S FIRST STANLEY CUP IN 47 YEARS.
2020
2021
ANDREI VASILEVSKIY RECORDS A SHUTOUT IN GAME 5 TO SECURE BACK-TO-BACK CUPS FOR THE TAMPA BAY LIGHTNING.
2023

CHAMPIONSHIP FACTS

STANELY CUP FINAL

First awarded: 1893

First modern Stanley Cup Final: 1927

Most titles as a player: Henri Richard, 11

Most titles as a coach: Scotty Bowman, 9

Most titles by a team: Montreal Canadiens, 23

Stats are accurate through the 2022–23 season.

MORE INFORMATION

To learn more about the Stanley Cup, go to **pressboxbooks.com/AllAccess**.

These links are routinely monitored and updated to provide the most current information available.

GLOSSARY

amateur
Having to do with players who are not paid.

captain
A player who serves as the leader of a team.

dynasty
A team that has an extended period of success, usually winning multiple championships in the process.

elite
The best of the best.

hat trick
When a player scores three or more goals in a game.

postseason
A tournament for qualified teams after the regular season is over; another term for playoffs.

rookie
A first-year player.

salary cap
The upper limit of how much a team is allowed to pay all of its players.

traditions
Ways of doing things that are passed down over many years.

two-way
Skilled at both offensive and defensive play.

INDEX